HAVE YOU HEARD ABOUT EPIC! YET?

We're the largest digital library for kids, used by millions in homes and schools around the world. We love stories so much that we're now creating our own!

With the help of some of the best writers and illustrators in the world, we create the wildest adventures we can think of. Like a mermaid and narwhal who solve mysteries. Or a pet made out of slime.

We hope you have as much fun reading our books as we h

epic! originals

BARK PARK

BRANDI DOUGHERTY
ILLUSTRATED BY PAIGE POOLER

Andrews McMeel
PUBLISHING®

CHAPTER 1

BARK PARK

THE POPPED BALL

It was a beautiful day at Bark Park. The sun shone brightly, but it wasn't too hot. A nice breeze blew through, making Scout's large, fawn-colored ears twitch. It was the perfect day to sit in the shade and munch on blueberries, Scout's absolute favorite snack. *And maybe, just maybe,* she thought, *a mystery might pop up.*

Scout came to the dog park every day, and all the dogs knew her. She was the smallest dog in the park, but what Scout lacked in size, she made up for in smarts. Scout was something of a dog detective. And, as luck would have it, Bark Park always seemed to have a mystery that needed solving.

Scout stood on a bench, eating blueberries from a little tin bowl and surveying the dogs who had already gathered in a large, dusty

play spot.
Maggie, the
Goldendoodle,
was lying on
her back
with her

favorite ball in her mouth. Her
legs kicked in the air like she was
dancing upside down.

"Thish ish the besth," Maggie
said around the ball. Maggie was
rarely without a ball of some kind,
but the red squishy plastic
one was her favorite.

Maggie bicycled her legs one more time and then jumped up and ran in wide circles at top speed. Even on the hottest summer day, when every other dog was panting in the shade or slurping from the water fountain, Maggie had endless energy. How she managed that was one mystery Scout couldn't solve.

A few feet from Maggie, in the shade of the biggest tree in Bark Park, lay Gus. Gus's large jowls were spread in the dirt as he

snored through his short, wide nose. He was an English bulldog who had buried more toys than he could count, and he was by far the oldest dog at the park.

Sprinkles entered through the gate, growling at a dog who was taking too long to get inside. Then he walked over and barked, "Hey Maggie, how about a turn with your ball?"

Maggie opened her mouth to reply, and the ball fell to the ground and rolled over to Gus.

She leaped over and pounced on the ball, accidentally knocking into the old bulldog and waking him from his nap.

"Not right now, Sprinkles," Maggie told the little terrier. She picked up the ball and jogged over to the fence.

"Maggie never shares," Sprinkles huffed. He turned and scratched his back paws in the dirt to kick up dust in her direction.

Rocky sat down next to

Sprinkles and licked his paw. "But it's Maggie's ball," he pointed out. His eyes grew big and serious. "You don't want to get in trouble with Maggie's human."

"You know, Maggie's ball looks a lot like my ball," Gus said as he yawned in his spot under the tree. "I have a red ball, too, and I don't see it."

Scout's ears perked in Gus's direction. If Gus's ball was missing, there might be a mystery to solve.

Suddenly, Maggie dropped her ball and raised her head, sniffing the air. "TREATS!" she barked. All of the dogs turned at once. Maggie's human was known for bringing treats for everyone. She sat on a bench near the park entrance with an open bag of Pooch Puffs.

Dogs ran toward her from every direction. They barked with excitement, waiting for their snacks.

Once the treat bag was empty, the dogs went back to the dusty play spot—except Maggie, who had spotted her ball near the fence. But it didn't look the same. It was popped. Out of air. Flat as a pancake.

"My ball!" she cried. "Who popped my ball?" Maggie jumped in a circle around the sad lump of red plastic. The other dogs began to gather nearby.

Scout's eyes widened. *A mystery.* She walked slowly to the center of the circle. She was calm. She was cool. She would handle this. She opened her mouth to speak.

A tiny burp came out.

"Excuse me." Scout gave a low growl to clear her throat.

"Errr, what's the problem, Maggie?"

Maggie was still doing laps around her deflated toy. She stopped every third or fourth time around to poke the ball with her nose. "Someone popped my favorite red ball! Look—there are teeth marks!"

"Hmmm, I see," Scout said.

"Maybe Sprinkles did it!" Maggie barked, fixing her eyes on the small terrier at the edge of the circle. "He wanted my ball."

"I was getting a treat, just like everyone else!" Sprinkles protested.

Scout looked closely at Sprinkles. Then she turned back to Maggie and inspected the ball. The teeth marks had been left by a dog with big, widely spaced teeth.

"Do you think it could have been Gus?" Rocky asked, looking unsure about calling out the old bulldog. "He thought Maggie's ball was his. Maybe he took it by mistake!"

Scout turned in Gus's direction. As Gus shifted in the dirt, Scout caught sight of something round in a hole in the ground under his leg.

She turned her attention back to the popped ball. There was a small scrap of tinfoil in the dirt next to it. She glanced around the park again, and then up into the trees.

Scout cleared her throat. "These teeth marks are too big to have been made by Sprinkles. Plus, he has crumbs on his nose.

He must have been getting treats from Maggie's human when the ball was popped."

"I told you it wasn't me," Sprinkles grumbled as he licked his nose clean.

"The teeth marks could have come from Gus, but he didn't leave his spot under the tree, and I can see his red ball under his leg. If he'd gotten up, he definitely would have found his own ball, not Maggie's," Scout said.

Gus turned his head to look

beneath his leg. "Hey, I found my ball!" he snorted.

"I think the teeth marks are from you, Maggie, because I know you like to chew on the ball, but you never pop it," Scout said.

Maggie nodded. "Okay, so then what happened?" she asked.

Her ears drooped low against her head.

Scout turned to look at the trees one more time. She walked in a slow circle, waiting until the dogs had all stopped barking. They sat, tails thumping, waiting for her to speak. "I believe it might ha...HICCUP! Excuse me. I believe it might have been Abigail, the crow," she finally announced.

The other dogs gasped in surprise just as Abigail let out a

loud *CAW!* Scout flipped the ball over, revealing another tiny set of holes. "Abigail likes to collect shiny things. This piece of tinfoil must have gotten stuck to the ball when Maggie dropped it to get her treat. Abigail could have swooped down to grab the tinfoil but popped the ball and got scared off, instead."

Abigail cawed again. "Sorry, Maggie!"

"Well done, Scout!" the dogs all barked at once.

Scout nodded and headed back to her bench. Her human came over and poured out a big pile of blueberries. Scout lapped up the berries hungrily. She didn't want a nosy bird to get to them first!

CHAPTER 2

BARK PARK

THE CONE OF SHAME

Scout walked in the gate of Bark Park and looked around. She was early. Only Gus and Walter were there. Walter liked to tease other dogs and always had a trick up his paw. Rumor had it that he lived in the house behind the park, but no one ever saw his human or knew exactly where he'd come from. He just sort of appeared each day.

As Scout watched Walter chewing on an old rope toy, she

wondered if maybe today was the day to crack The Mystery of Where Walter Came From. But something else caught her eye. It was Rocky.

Walter stopped chewing and watched Rocky, too. The sight made him howl with laughter.

Rocky was a *very* large dog, but he didn't usually have trouble getting into the park. However, today something was hanging around his neck. And whatever it was kept getting caught on the

edge of the gate, pushing Rocky backward when he tried to move forward.

Gus lifted his jowls from the dirt and squinted at the gate. "What is Rocky wearing?"

Walter rolled sideways in the dirt, laughing. "A cone of shame! He's wearing a cone of shame!"

Scout frowned. "Walter, don't be mean."

With some help from his human, Rocky finally made it into the park, head drooping with embarrassment. But then the bottom edge of the cone caught on a mound of dirt and he tipped forward. Rocky fell face-first onto the ground, and his tail flipped in the air.

Maggie bounced into the park. "Rocky, are you okay?" She shifted from paw to paw.

Scout walked over and dug away some of the dirt in front of the cone so Rocky could sit up. "I...I think so," Rocky said. He scratched at the gauze tie keeping the cone firmly around his neck.

"Why are you wearing that?" Scout asked.

Rocky shook his head. "I'm not sure. My paw has been bothering me a little, but my head is fine! When I woke up this morning, the cone was already on."

"Hmmm," Scout mumbled. *A mystery.* She walked in a tight circle around Rocky, examining the plastic cone from every angle as the big dog scratched at it.

It didn't look like it was going anywhere.

"I just want it off!" Rocky groaned. "I keep running into things, and I can't even get a drink of water."

Walter came over to the group. "I might know a guy."

Rocky squinted at him. "A guy?" he asked.

"Well, you know, a dog," Walter said. "In the alley." He motioned toward the back alley with his nose. "He can help get that thing off."

Rocky backed up a step, stumbling over his own paws and landing on his butt. "I don't know," he said. "I've never been to the alley before."

"You'll probably disappear and never come back." Sprinkles

was frowning. "And then we'll have to look for you, and I won't get my morning nap."

"Why are you always so grumpy, Sprinkles?" Maggie asked.

"You'd be grumpy, too, if you were kept up every night listening to the wails of a tiny human," Sprinkles mumbled.

Rocky paced around until his cone hit the bench, pushing him backward. "Is it the only way?" he asked Walter.

Walter nodded. "Unless anyone else has a better idea?"

No one spoke up. Even though they wanted to help Rocky, none of them knew how to wriggle out of a *cone of shame.*

Rocky gave a long sigh. "Okay,

fine. I'll go—if you're sure it's safe."

Walter led the way to the back fence as Rocky, Maggie, Sprinkles, and Scout followed. Scout glanced at the humans, but they were engaged in a lively debate about where to put a new water fountain. She just hoped her human would wait to put out her blueberries. Otherwise, Tippy the squirrel might steal them all.

Walter led them to a section of fence where the boards were loose. He pushed the boards aside and Rocky backed out through the opening so his cone wouldn't get caught. The other dogs followed.

The alley was fully in the shade. It felt a lot colder and

darker than the dog park. There were some empty boxes and big dumpsters. Judy, the local stray cat, sat on top of one of the dumpsters licking a mostly empty tuna can.

A large brown-and-black dog with a thick tail walked out from behind a stack of boxes.

"Hi, Bones." Walter stepped forward and spoke in a hushed whisper. The two dogs looked back at Rocky. Rocky's eyes darted nervously to Scout, who

gave Rocky an encouraging smile.

Bones stood in front of Rocky. "What's the cone for?"

"I'm not sure," Rocky said. "My human was on the phone with the vet yesterday, and my paw has been a little itchy. But I don't know what that could have to do with this thing!"

"Huh. Well, this is how it's going to happen," Bones said. "When I step on the top of the cone, you pull your head back—hard."

Scout's big ears twitched. She knew this plan wasn't going to work. The gauze was tied too tight. But before she could tell Rocky, he had lowered his head to the pavement. Bones placed his

two front paws on the plastic cone.
Rocky put all of his weight on his
back legs and pulled. The cone
pushed against his ears. All the
skin and fur on his face smushed
forward, covering his eyes. He
pulled and tugged and tugged
and pulled, but nothing happened.

"Huh," Bones said. "I thought
for sure that would work." He
took his paws off the cone and
Rocky flew backward, knocking
over a tower of boxes.

Rocky hung his head and

shuffled back toward the dog park. "I'm going to be stuck in this thing forever," he moaned.

"No way. We'll figure out how to get that cone off, Rocky!" Scout said.

Scout, Maggie, and Sprinkles followed Rocky, while Walter stayed behind with Bones.

Once they were back in Bark Park, Scout walked around Rocky again, studying the cone. "Oh, I get it now," she said as she traced the loops of gauze around the

plastic cone. The gauze ended in a pretty little bow. Scout nodded to herself. "I think I know how to get it off."

"You do?" the other three dogs barked together.

Scout nodded. Then she hiccupped. "Excuse me. I mean, yes, I do," she said. "Lie down, Rocky."

Rocky flattened to the dirt. Scout dragged over an empty water bowl and tipped it upside down. When she stood on it, she was just able to reach Rocky's neck. She put her front paws on his shoulder and nudged the gauze tie with her nose until she found the end. Then she grabbed the end in her teeth, stepped off the bowl, and walked slowly backward until the tie came loose. Rocky gave his head a quick jerk, and the cone fell right off.

"I'm free! I'm free!" Rocky barked. He ran in a circle, shaking his head and enjoying how it felt to flop his ears around again. He headed right over to the water fountain and got a long drink from the bowl underneath. Then he started running in circles again.

Scout and the other dogs watched Rocky's dance of freedom. But it stopped just as quickly as it had started. Before anyone knew what was happening, Rocky plopped down in the dirt and started furiously licking his paw.

"Rocky? What are you doing?" Sprinkles asked.

"My paw...is...so...itchy," he said between licks and nipping bites.

Scout narrowed her eyes and walked over to inspect Rocky's paw. There was a big sore patch right between his toes. "Oh, I see! No wonder you were wearing the cone of shame, Rocky. You have a sore on your paw."

"Maybe that's why my human

was on the phone with the vet. She was worried about my paw!" Just then, Rocky's human walked up and slid the cone right back over his head. "No licking!" she said, tying it tight.

"Well..." Scout shook her head. "Mystery solved."

CHAPTER 3

BARK PARK

THE MISSING BONE

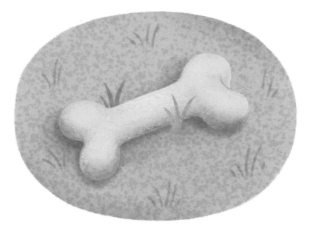

The day started like any other day. Scout woke up, ate her breakfast with a side of blueberries, and walked to Bark Park with her human. When she arrived, nothing seemed strange or out of the ordinary, except for

Gus, who was digging in the dirt instead of sleeping. Maggie was running the length of the park, tossing her new ball up in the air and catching it as she ran. Rocky was fumbling around, trying to figure out how to lick his paw around the cone of shame. And Sprinkles was prancing through the dirt, humming to himself.

Scout stopped her survey of the park. Sprinkles was in a good mood! He was never in a good mood. Scout grinned. *A mystery!*

A dog in the corner of the park barked at the fence, which made Scout turn and look. At the top of the fence sat Tippy. The nosy squirrel was often mistaken for a small dog because she was almost the size of one. She also loved to steal dog treats—and Scout's blueberries!

Scout was about to ask Sprinkles why he was in such a good mood when Gus gave a frustrated grunt. "What's up, Gus?" Scout asked.

Gus stood next to what was now a very large hole. "My bone is gone! I buried it right here yesterday. But now it's missing!"

Scout stood at the edge of the hole and peered inside. "Hmmm. Are you sure that's where you buried it, Gus?"

Gus nodded, his jowls shaking. "I'm sure. At least, I think so..."

Maggie bounded to a stop in front of them. "I'll helpth you looth for your bone, Gush," she said with her ball in her mouth.

"I'll help, too," Scout said. After all, a missing bone was definitely a mystery!

Scout started her investigation by studying the hole at Gus's feet. The dirt was a bit damp—not dusty and dry, like most of the park. The dirt on Gus's paws looked like mud. Scout put her nose down as she walked, looking at the toes of the other dogs in the park. Their paws were dusty, but not muddy. Scout went over to where Sprinkles lay in the shade with a smile on his face. The dirt on his paws was muddy, just like the dirt on Gus's. *Interesting.*

Meanwhile, Maggie and Rocky had started digging holes near the one Gus had made. As

they dug, Scout surveyed the scene. She kept an eye out for the bone and watched Sprinkles at the same time. His good mood and the mud on his paws were definitely suspicious. "How are you today, Sprinkles?" Scout asked, her eyes zeroing in on the dog's face.

"Great! I'm great!" Sprinkles replied.

"And why is that?" Scout asked.

"Because—"

"HELP!" Scout and Sprinkles looked around to see who was crying out. It didn't take them long to find Rocky stuck facedown in the hole he'd just dug!

Scout and Sprinkles rushed to help, but there wasn't much the little dogs could do. Maggie and

Gus were bigger, and they were able to get Rocky's head unstuck.

"Thanks." Rocky sneezed, dirt clinging to his nose. "I hope I'm not getting a cold!"

"Did you find my bone?" Gus asked.

"No," Rocky said. "But I did find a cat collar and half a tennis ball."

"I'll take the tennis ball!" Maggie said, grabbing it out of the hole. "I want it for my collection."

Tippy chattered from the fence above them.

"Have you seen my bone?" Gus asked her.

Tippy shoved a stolen Pooch Puff into her mouth. "Nope." And with that, she jumped off the fence and scampered up the tree.

Maggie, Gus, and Rocky went back to digging holes. Sprinkles

went back to prancing about in the dirt. Scout studied the tree for a minute. Then she looked around the park. Sprinkles was still a suspect, but she had another lead, too. Just to be sure, she approached Sprinkles again. "Why are you in such a good mood today?" she asked.

Gus stopped digging and looked up.

"Who, me?" Sprinkles asked innocently. By now, Rocky and Maggie had stopped digging, too, and were listening to the conversation.

"Yes," Scout nodded. "You. I haven't seen you this happy in a while."

"Good point, Scout," Gus snorted.

"Well, it just so happens that today I have an appointment at the groomer," Sprinkles said.

Maggie shuddered. "And that makes you…happy?"

Sprinkles smiled again. "It does."

"Why on earth would that make you happy?" Maggie asked, looking shocked.

"Because it means that after I leave here, I go straight to the groomer's without going home.

I get an entire day away from the monster," Sprinkles said with a shudder.

"A monster? Where?" Rocky asked, looking around.

"The baby at my house. The one-year-old with the sticky, grabby hands and all that drool! But today, I get a whole day of peace and quiet."

Scout grinned. "Well, that solves *that* mystery!"

"So if Sprinkles didn't take my bone, who did?" asked Gus.

"Maybe we should be asking *what*, not *who*," Scout said.

"Huh?" the other dogs barked at the same time.

Scout walked quickly around the holes her friends had dug. "You see...," she started, but then she tripped and landed in one of the holes. She scrambled out, trying to look serious. "It appears as though the water fountain has been moved."

Scout stopped next to a hole where the water fountain used to be. Then she walked (more carefully this time) to the other side of the tree near the fence, where the new water fountain now stood. The ground around it looked freshly moved and repacked. "Could this be where you buried your bone, Gus?"

Gus blew a breath through

his short nose. "Well, it sure could be. That sure looks like the spot."

"Then I'm afraid you'll have to get a new bone because yours is buried under the fountain! Unless..." Scout walked around the back of the fountain and looked at the space between it and the fence. There, in the mound of fresh dirt, sat the bone.

"Well done as usual, Scout!" Maggie barked.

Scout was pleased. Two

mysteries solved in one day! Now to see about a well-deserved blueberry snack and that cat collar that Rocky had dug up...

MORE TO EXPLORE

DO CROWS LIKE SHINY THINGS?

In "The Popped Ball," Abigail, the crow, can't resist a piece of tinfoil. But do *all* crows love to pick up shiny objects?

Crows belong to a family of birds called corvids, which also includes magpies and ravens. Young corvids are very curious (much like young humans!), making them especially drawn to bright, shiny objects.

As they fly, crows can spot reflective items like tinfoil easily, and their curiosity often leads them to swoop down and pick up the shiny objects they see. In fact, a young girl in Seattle made a whole collection of beads and colored glass that crows dropped in her yard after she fed them.

WHY DO DOGS WEAR CONES?

In "The Cone of Shame," poor Rocky comes to the dog park wearing a cone on his head. Cones like these are very common, so maybe you've seen one. While they can make pets feel uncomfortable, they prevent them from scratching or licking an injured part of their body. Once the injury heals, the owner or veterinarian removes the cone.

Cones can be made of plastic or fabric, and with a little practice, most animals can still eat and drink while wearing them. It can be strange to see an animal wearing a cone, but think of it like a special bandage. And the best part: When the cone comes off, it means the pet is healthy!

WHAT DOES A PET GROOMER DO?

In "The Missing Bone," Sprinkles is happy because he will be going to the groomer. At the groomer's, dogs might get their fur shampooed and brushed, their nails trimmed, and their ears cleaned. Some dogs might even get a fancy hairstyle with ribbons. It's like a spa for our furry friends.

Some pet groomers go to a special school to learn how to do their jobs. Being a groomer requires patience and care, since not all pets like to be bathed and have their nails clipped. We humans need to bathe, clip our nails, and brush our hair to stay healthy, and so do our furry pals!

ABOUT THE AUTHOR

Brandi Dougherty was born and raised in Kalispell, Montana. After earning an English degree at Linfield College, she spent eight years working in children's publishing at Scholastic before moving to California, where she pursued writing and freelance editing full-time. Brandi now calls sunny Los Angeles her home, where she wrangles two adorable kids and one crazy dog with her husband, Joe.

ABOUT THE ILLUSTRATOR

Paige Pooler has worked for twenty-five years as a children's illustrator and character designer for print, online, and television media. She has illustrated numerous children's chapter books, book covers, greeting cards, stickers, and product art. Paige currently lives in Los Angeles, California, with her two very smart and adorable rescue dogs. When she's not working or doodling, she likes to hike the local hills, search for the best taco trucks, and plot her next travel adventure.

Andrews McMeel Publishing
a division of Andrews McMeel Universal
1130 Walnut Street, Kansas City, Missouri 64106

www.andrewsmcmeel.com

Epic! Creations, Inc.
702 Marshall Street, Suite 280, Redwood City, California 94063

www.getepic.com

20 21 22 23 24 SDB 10 9 8 7 6 5 4 3 2 1

Paperback ISBN: 978-1-5248-5824-7
Hardback ISBN: 978-1-5248-6042-4

Library of Congress Control Number: 2019954707

Photo credits: page 83, maqtiriri/Shutterstock.com
page 85, Mary Swift/Shutterstock.com
page 87, hedgehog94/Shutterstock.com

Design by Dan Nordskog

Made by:
King Yip (Dongguan) Printing & Packaging Factory Ltd.
Address and location of manufacturer:
Daning Administrative District, Humen Town
Dongguan Guangdong, China 523930
1st Printing — 2/3/20

ATTENTION: SCHOOLS AND BUSINESSES
Andrews McMeel books are available at quantity
discounts with bulk purchase for educational, business,
or sales promotional use. For information, please
e-mail the Andrews McMeel Publishing Special Sales
Department: specialsales@amuniversal.com.